Snowman Paul
returns to the WINTER OLYMPICS

Written by **YOSSI LAPID** • Illustrated by **JOANNA PASEK**

Art Direction & Design by **RICHARD BRUNING**

LAPID CHILDREN'S BOOKS

"Hey," cried Paul. "Come quick and see,
I'm asked to be a referee,

At the Olympics, in support
Of truth and honesty in sport!"

Look, I must study
all of this!

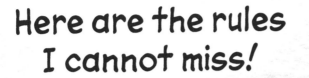

Here are the rules
I cannot miss!

The Referee
Handbook

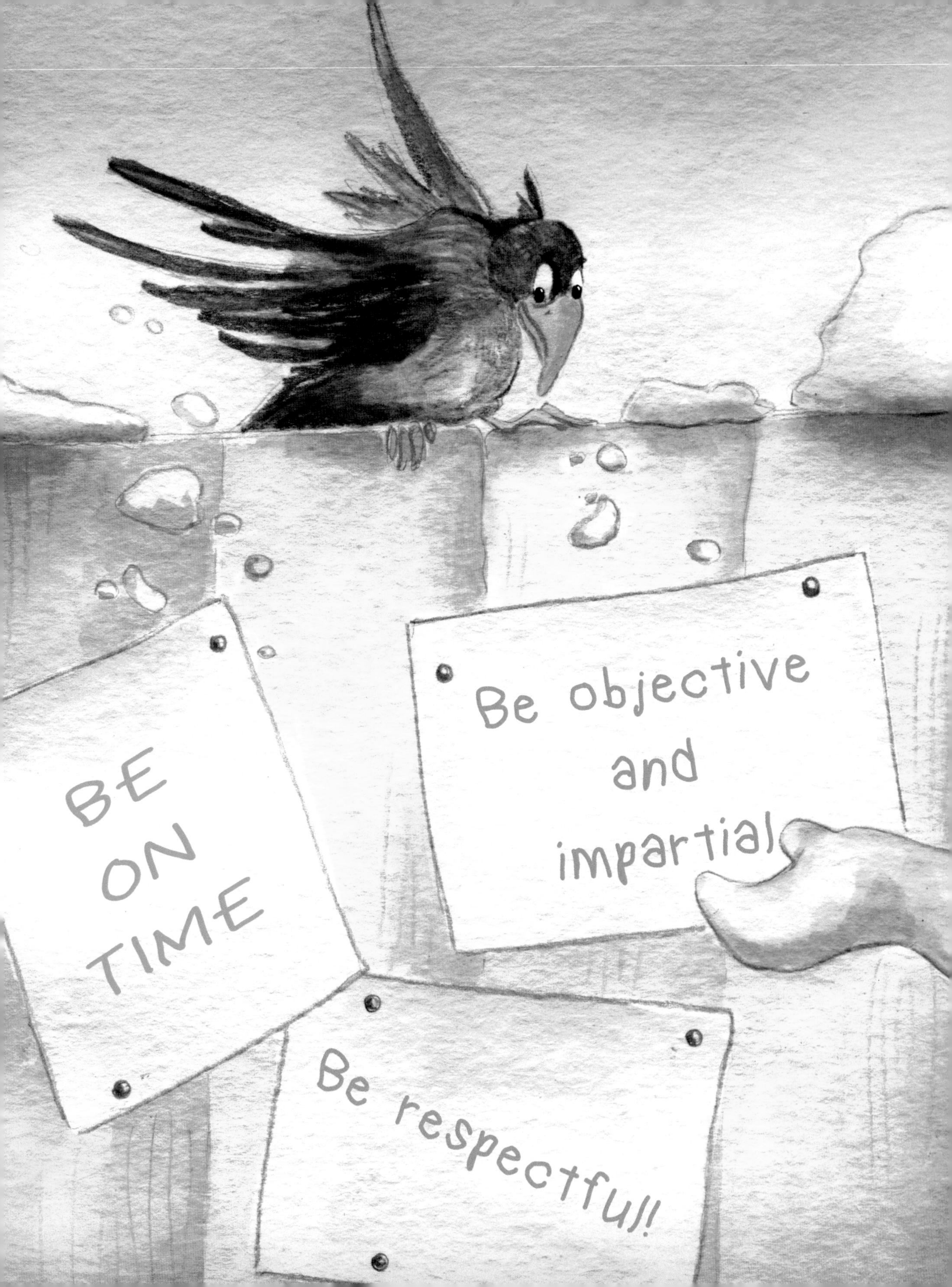
BE ON TIME
Be objective and impartial
Be respectful!

5 things
to remember
3 GOOD
HABITS
OF
OLYMPIC
REFEREES
ALPIN
SKII
RULES
OF
HOCK
Figure
Skating
Jumps
Speed skating
Figure skating
Ski Jumping
Ice Hockey

"Don't know,"
said Paul.

Soon, everything began to change,
And life became a little strange.

My friends and I
still had great fun,

But Paul was always on the run!

Then, when we all played hide and seek,

I saw Paul take a sneaky peek.

He inched closer
day by day.

At last, he asked, "Dan, may *I* play?"

"But don't you need to referee?"

"No more," said Paul.
"It's not for *me!*

It's boring and I miss the fun...
I'd love to play with everyone!"

We took our friends
along with us

And boarded the
Olympic bus.

My Paul was honored all the same,
And carried the Olympic flame.

But when the games
came to an end,

I knew that Paul
was my *true* friend!

*To Lila with love
and gratitude.*

DEAR READER

Thank you for reading SNOWMAN PAUL RETURNS TO THE WINTER OLYMPICS!

*If you like this book, please take a moment to post
a review on Amazon and/or Goodreads.*

*Your support makes a big difference, and helps other readers
discover and enjoy Snowman Paul's exciting and humorous adventures.*

*Visit our website, lapidchildrensbooks.com to learn
about new books, special offers and informative newsletters.*

And, if you sign up for our mailing list, you will receive a special FREE GIFT!

—In gratitude, Yossi

Lapid Children's Books is
an independent publisher of
memorable and beautifully
produced picture books that
celebrate childhood and inspire
a love of reading and life-long
learning at an early age.

LAPID CHILDREN'S BOOKS

Yossi Lapid is the author of the
award-winning *Snowman Paul,
Sasha* and *Yara* book series.
He has three children and he lives
with his wife, Susan, in New Mexico.

Joanna Pasek is an award-winning
children's book illustrator from
Poland. She lives with her family
near Crakow.

SNOWMAN PAUL

On a snowy winter day, **Dan** builds himself a friendly snowman, but his joy is spoiled when **Bill**, the neighborhood bully, makes fun of him. **Snowman Paul** magically comes alive and, as Dan's new best friend, helps him overcome his fears. Beautifully illustrated, this rhyming series has earned multiple awards and over **600 five-star reviews** on Amazon. Join **Snowman Paul** and **Dan** in their exciting and engaging adventures!

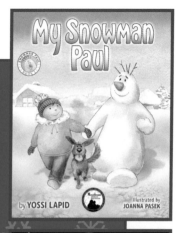

My Snowman Paul
by YOSSI LAPID
Illustrated by JOANNA PASEK

Valentine's Day with Snowman Paul
by YOSSI LAPID
Illustrated by JOANNA PASEK

The Amazing Snowman Duel
by YOSSI LAPID
Illustrated by JOANNA PASEK

Christmas with Snowman Paul
by YOSSI LAPID
Illustrated by JOANNA PASEK

Snowman Paul returns to the Winter Olympics
by YOSSI LAPID
Illustrated by JOANNA PASEK

Halloween with Snowman Paul
by YOSSI LAPID
Illustrated by JOANNA PASEK

Snowman Paul at the Concert Hall
by YOSSI LAPID
Illustrated by JOANNA PASEK

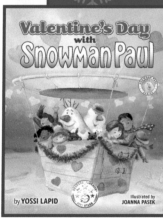

Valentine's Day with Snowman Paul
by YOSSI LAPID
Illustrated by JOANNA PASEK

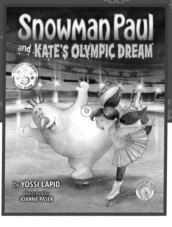

Snowman Paul and Kate's Olympic Dream
by YOSSI LAPID
Illustrated by JOANNA PASEK

Mother's Day with Snowman Paul
by YOSSI LAPID
Illustrated by JOANNA PASEK

SASHA THE LUCKY PUPPY

Sasha is a lucky puppy! He has his **"Big Boss" Bob**, an experienced and loving dog owner who is not always perfect. He has **Joy, Bob's little sister**, who is adorable but is only now learning how to take care of a pet. And he has an **adventure-filled** life which he is eager to share with you.

Written from the perspective of a precocious puppy, this series shows that it is not always easy being a pet, even when you have a **wonderful life!**

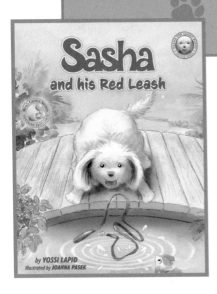

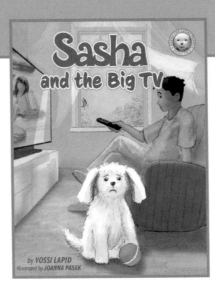

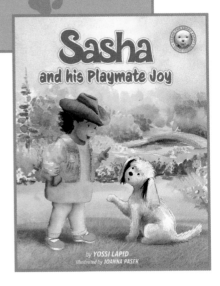

YARA'S RAINFOREST

Yara lives with her **Mama** in the lush **Amazon jungle**. She wants to save her beloved but increasingly besieged **rainforest home**. With heartwarming rhyming stories and absolutely remarkable artwork, this **award-winning** book series offers perfect openings for discussions on the environment.

Join **Yara** in her timely efforts to save our **beautiful planet!**